How the
Elephant
got its Trunk

Retold by Robert James

Illustrated by Garyfallia Leftheri

Crabtree Publishing Company

www.crabtreebooks.com

Crabtree Publishing Company
www.crabtreebooks.com
1-800-387-7650

PMB 59051, 350 Fifth Ave.
59th Floor,
New York, NY 10118

616 Welland Ave.
St. Catharines, ON
L2M 5V6

Published by Crabtree Publishing in 2012
Printed in the U.S.A./052012/FA20120413

Series editor: Jackie Hamley
Editor: Kathy Middleton
Proofreader: Reagan Miller
Series advisor: Catherine Glavina
Series designer: Peter Scoulding
Print and Production coordinator:
  Katherine Berti

Text © Franklin Watts 2010
Printed in Canada/072014/MA20140616

The rights of Robert James to be identified as the author and Garyfallia Leftheri as the illustrator of this Work have been asserted.

First published in 2010
by Franklin Watts
(A division of Hachette
Children's Books)

**Library and Archives Canada
Cataloguing in Publication**

CIP available at Library and Archives Canada

**Library of Congress
Cataloging-in-Publication Data**

CIP available at Library of Congress

This story tries to explain some of the different things we see in the world today. It was originally written by an author called Rudyard Kipling, over 100 years ago.

Long ago, the Elephant had a short nose.

3

Baby Elephant
was always asking
questions.

One day, he asked,
"What does Crocodile
eat for dinner?"

Nobody would tell him.

So Baby Elephant
asked Bird.

"Go to the river and find out!" replied Bird.

There, Baby Elephant saw an animal that looked like a log.

"Are you Crocodile?"
he asked.

"Yes!" said Crocodile.

"What do you eat
for dinner?" asked
Baby Elephant.

"Come closer,
and I'll tell you,"
smiled Crocodile.

Crocodile bit
Baby Elephant's
short nose.

"Help!" cried
Baby Elephant.

Baby Elephant
pulled and pulled.

His nose got
longer and longer.

19

And that is how
the Elephant got
its long trunk!

Puzzle Time!

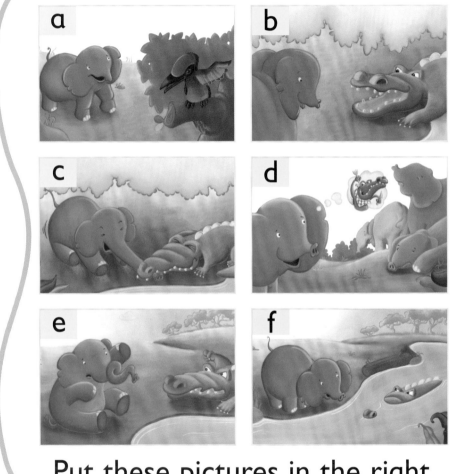

Put these pictures in the right order and tell the story!

curious

sly

nosy

clever

Which words describe Baby Elephant and which describe Crocodile?

Turn the page for the answers!

Notes for adults

TADPOLES: TALES are structured for emergent readers. The books may also be used for read-alouds or shared reading with young children.

How the Elephant got its Trunk is based on a classic story by Rudyard Kipling. This kind of story is known as a "just-so" or "porquoi" story because it explains how something came to be. For example, many of Kipling's stories explain how certain animals developed their unique characteristics. Since young children are often curious and filled with questions, "just-so" stories make ideal reading material.

IF YOU ARE READING THIS BOOK WITH A CHILD, HERE ARE A FEW SUGGESTIONS:

1. Make reading fun! Choose a time to read when you and the child are relaxed and have time to share the story.

2. Explain that the story is called a "just so" or "pourquoi" story. *Pourquoi* is a French word that means "why." Pourquoi stories are tales that explain why or how something is in the world. This information will help set a purpose for reading.

3. Encourage the child to reread the story and to retell it using his or her own words. Invite the child to use the illustrations as a guide.

4. Encourage the child to use his or her imagination to think of other "just-so" story topics. What "why" or "how" questions about animals can they think of?

5. Give praise! Children learn best in a positive environment.

HERE ARE OTHER TITLES FROM TADPOLES: TALES FOR YOU TO ENJOY:

How the Camel got his Hump	978-0-7787-7888-2 RLB	978-0-7787-7900-1 PB
The Ant and the Grasshopper	978-0-7787-7889-9 RLB	978-0-7787-7901-8 PB
The Boy who cried Wolf	978-0-7787-7890-5 RLB	978-0-7787-7902-5 PB
The Fox and the Crow	978-0-7787-7892-9 RLB	978-0-7787-7904-9 PB
The Lion and the Mouse	978-0-7787-7893-6 RLB	978-0-7787-7905-6 PB

VISIT WWW.CRABTREEBOOKS.COM FOR OTHER CRABTREE BOOKS.

Answers

Here is the correct order!
1. d 2. a 3. f 4. b 5. c 6. e

Words to describe Baby Elephant:
curious, nosy

Words to describe Crocodile:
clever, sly